W9-CMI-822

NIAGARA FALLS PUBLIC LIBRARY

Skateboarding

A Level Two Reader

By Cynthia Klingel and Robert B. Noyed

The Child's World®

Skateboarding is a fun sport. It looks easy, but it takes time to learn.

You need to wear a helmet,
kneepads, and wrist guards.
They help keep you safe
when you fall.

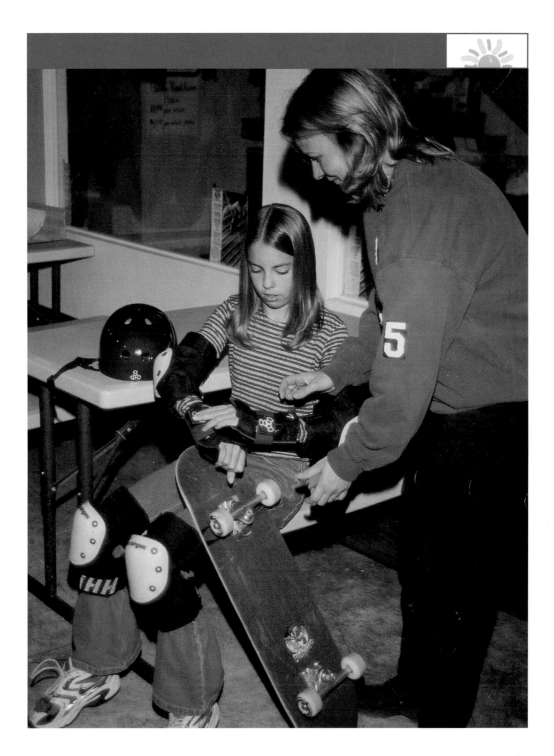

5

The skateboard tips from side to side. You hold out your arms to keep your balance.

When you lean to the right or left, the skateboard turns. Turning on a skateboard is tricky.

You are ready to go faster. You need to push with your foot. Do not go too fast or you will fall.

Some kids can do
skateboarding tricks.
It takes a lot of practice.

Kyle jumps in the air.

It looks as if the skateboard

is stuck to his feet.

He rides his board on the ramp. He races down one side and up the other.

16

18

Kyle is a really good skateboarder. He can do many tricks.

You can learn to skateboard, too. It takes a lot of practice.

Index

To Find Out More

Books

Hills, Gavin. *Skateboarding.* Minneapolis: Lerner Publications Co., 1993.

Web Sites

Chairman of the Board: Tony Hawk
http://sikids.com/locker/hawk/
This site, sponsored by Sports Illustrated for Kids, provides information about skateboarder Tony Hawk and offers videos of his favorite tricks.

Chuck's Skate Place
http:/ww.sapskateboards.com/chuck/index.htm
Links to skate parks, equipment, and other information.

Skateboard Science
http://www.exploratorium.edu/skateboarding/
Information about skateboarding tricks, equipment, and terms.

Note to Parents and Educators

Welcome to The Wonders of Reading™! These books provide text at three different levels for beginning readers to practice and strengthen their reading skills. Additionally, the use of nonfiction text provides readers the valuable opportunity to *read to learn*, not just to learn to read.

These leveled readers allow children to choose books at their level of reading confidence and performance. Level One books offer beginning readers simple language, word choice, and sentence structure as well as a word list. Level Two books feature slightly more difficult vocabulary, longer sentences, and longer total text. In the back of each Level Two book are an index and a list of books and Web sites for finding out more information. Level Three books continue to extend word choice and length of text. In the back of each Level Three book are a glossary, an index, and a list of books and Web sites for further research.

State and national standards in reading and language arts emphasize using nonfiction at all levels of reading development. The Wonders of Reading™ fill the historical void in nonfiction material for the primary grade readers with the additional benefit of a leveled text.

About the Authors

Cindy Klingel has worked as a high school English teacher and an elementary teacher. She is currently the curriculum director for a Minnesota school district. Writing children's books is another way for her to continue her passion for sharing the written word with children. Cindy Klingel is a frequent visitor to the children's section of bookstores and enjoys spending time with her many friends, family, and two daughters.

Bob Noyed started his career as a newspaper reporter. Since then, he has worked in communications and public relations for more than fourteen years for a Minnesota school district. He enjoys writing books for children and finds that it brings a different feeling of challenge and accomplishment from other writing projects. He is an avid reader who also enjoys music, theater, traveling, and spending time with his wife, son, and daughter.

Readers should remember…
All sports carry a certain amount of risk. To reduce your risk while skateboarding, skate at your own level, wear all safety equipment, and use care and common sense. The publisher and author will take no responsibility or liability for injuries resulting from skateboarding.

Published by The Child's World®, Inc.
PO Box 326
Chanhassen, MN 55317-0326
800-599-READ
www.childsworld.com

With special thanks to the Motzko and Cleveland families, and the Ramp, Rail, and Roll Indoor Skate Park in Mundelein, IL, for providing the modeling and location for this book.

Photo Credits
All photos © Flanagan Publishing Services/Romie Flanagan

Project Coordination: Editorial Directions, Inc.
Photo Research: Alice K. Flanagan

Copyright © 2001 by The Child's World®, Inc.
All rights reserved. No part of this book may be
reproduced or utilized in any form or by any means
without written permission from the publisher.
Printed in the United States of America.

Library of Congress Cataloging-in-Publication Data
Klingel, Cynthia Fitterer.
Skateboarding / by Cynthia Klingel and Robert B. Noyed.
p. cm.
"Wonder books."
Summary: Simple text describes skateboarding, how and where it is done,
the equipment used, and safety precautions.
ISBN 1-56766-818-6 (lib. bdg. : alk. paper)
1. Skateboarding—Juvenile literature. [1. Skateboarding.]
I. Noyed, Robert B.   II. Title.

GV859.8 .K58   2000
796.22—dc21   99-057721

NIAGARA FALLS PUBLIC LIBRARY
2 0 NOV 2001

Skateboarding.
Klingel, C.

PRICE: $20.13 (ONF/in/v)